For Grandpa Len ~ S S

For Arthur ~ R W

tiger tales
5 River Road, Suite 128, Wilton, CT 06897
Published in the United States 2014
Originally published in Great Britain 2014
by Little Tiger Press
Text copyright © 2014 Steve Smallman
Illustrations copyright © 2014 Richard Watson
ISBN-13: 978-1-58925-155-7
ISBN-10: 1-58925-155-5
Printed in China
LTP/1400/0747/0913

For more insight and activities,
visit us at www.tigertalesbooks.com

Scowl

by
Steve Smallman

Illustrated by
Richard Watson

The
Daily Grumble

LOOK OUT!
There's a
sheep thief
about...

"Baaaa-humbug"

tiger tales

Grumpy Branch

It was a dreamy, sunbeamy day
in Cupcake Wood.

Birds sang sweetly, bunnies hopped
happily. And a big, brown, bumbling bear
sat behind a bush reading his newspaper.

Everyone was happy. Everyone except . . .

...Scowl.

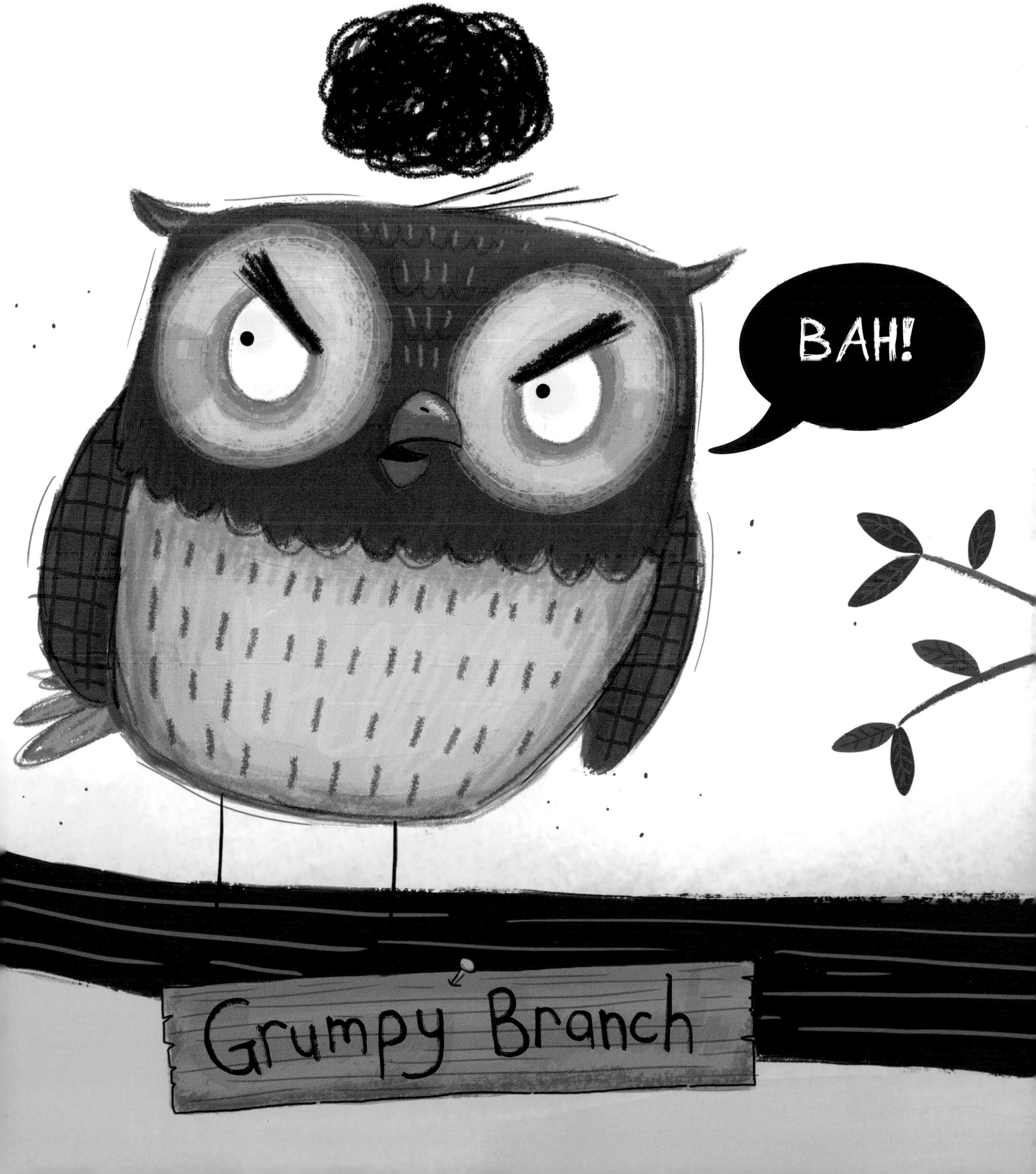
BAH!
Grumpy Branch

Scowl was grumpy no matter what the weather was like.

He was even grumpy
in his sleep.

The other animals decided
that **Scowl** needed cheering up.
One little bird had a great idea.

"You can wear my HAPPY HAT!" she twittered, plunking it on **Scowl's** head.

said **Scowl.**

"We just want you to be happy,
Scowl!" the animals cried.
But Scowl didn't give a hoot!

"Just leave me

alone, all of you!" he shouted.

Then he flew off to his
Grumpy Branch
for a bit of peace and quiet.
But when he got there ...

"I AM grumpy!"
screeched the little bird.

"Because YOU broke my
HAPPY HAT!"

Scowl felt funny. For the first time
in his life, he'd been out-grumped!
He flapped off, all embarrassed,
and rescued the happy hat.
Then he gave it to the
little bird and said . . .

Grumpy

"Does that hat *really* make
you happy?" asked Scowl.
"Yes!" twittered
the little bird.

Tee hee

Grumpy Branch

"But what makes *you* happy, Scowl?"
asked the other animals.
Scowl thought about it for a minute.
"Being grumpy!" he said. "It's great fun!"

"Hooray!" they all cried. "So we don't need to do *anything* to make you happy?"

"Well," said **Scowl**, "there is *one* thing that you could *all* do."

"What is it?" they asked eagerly.

And they did.